Rachel Bright & Debi Gliori

Side by Side

SCHOLASTIC INC.

Deep in the heart of Wintermouse Wood,

down in the grass where the autumn trees stood,

lived all kinds of creatures – some big and some small –

some spiky, some furry, some short, and some tall.

And here was a family of mouserly folk,
who nestled in burrow holes under an oak.

And the tiniest, weeniest, youngest of those,

who had sticky-out ears and a whiskerly nose,

was named Little Mouseling – she had a huge heart.

She loved times together, not ever apart.

But being so small, she was sometimes left out

when her brothers and sisters went up and about.

She would scurry and skip as fast as she could,

but they scattered so far across Wintermouse Wood.

"Wait for me!" she would sing. "Don't run! Oh, don't hide!

Is there nobody here who will stay by my side?"

Well, in Wintermouse Wood, you don't have to wait long . . .

. . . for one or another to answer your song.

"I'll stay by your side,
be a friend when you need!"
came the voice of Toad Flip,
who was down in the reeds.

"We could bounce up and down
and do backflips and jumps,
then plop in the water
and cool down our rumps!"

"How lovely," she said,
since she longed to dive in.
"I do like to bounce,
but . . .
this mouseling
can't swim."

From high in the branches, a voice echoed down.

"Well, then I'll be your friend!"

bellowed Big Squirrel Brown.

"We can pack up a picnic of hazelnut pie!

Go up side by side – till we're touching the sky!"

"You're too kind!" replied Mouseling.
"We'd have such a nice time.
And I do like nut pie,

but . . .

I'm too scared to climb."

Owl Hooty?

She wanted to soar through the sky,
but as everyone knows, of course,
mouselings can't fly.

Batty Fangs?

He wanted to stay up until dawn,

but even the thought of it made Mouseling yawn.

She stared at the sky with her eyes big and wide.

Would she ever find one who would stay by her side?

And as dark came in shadows and rain dropped in drips,
this mouseling ran out of her scurries and skips.

So she sat very quiet in her silvery fur –
no one seemed perfectly matching for her.

It seemed, in this world,
she was out on her own.
Deep in Wintermouse Wood,
she felt . . .

quite alone.

But someone had heard her side-by-side song.
Someone who'd been around all along.

He popped up his head from a very small hole –

a tinyful, weenimous, little black vole.

He was awfully quiet and terribly shy,

but he couldn't hear mouserly tears and stand by . . .

He peeped, "I'll be your friend!"

and he gave her a wink.

"Shall we dance ourselves happy?

What do you think?

We could make up some songs,"

he said, stroking his chin.

"Perhaps all of the Wood

will want to join in!"

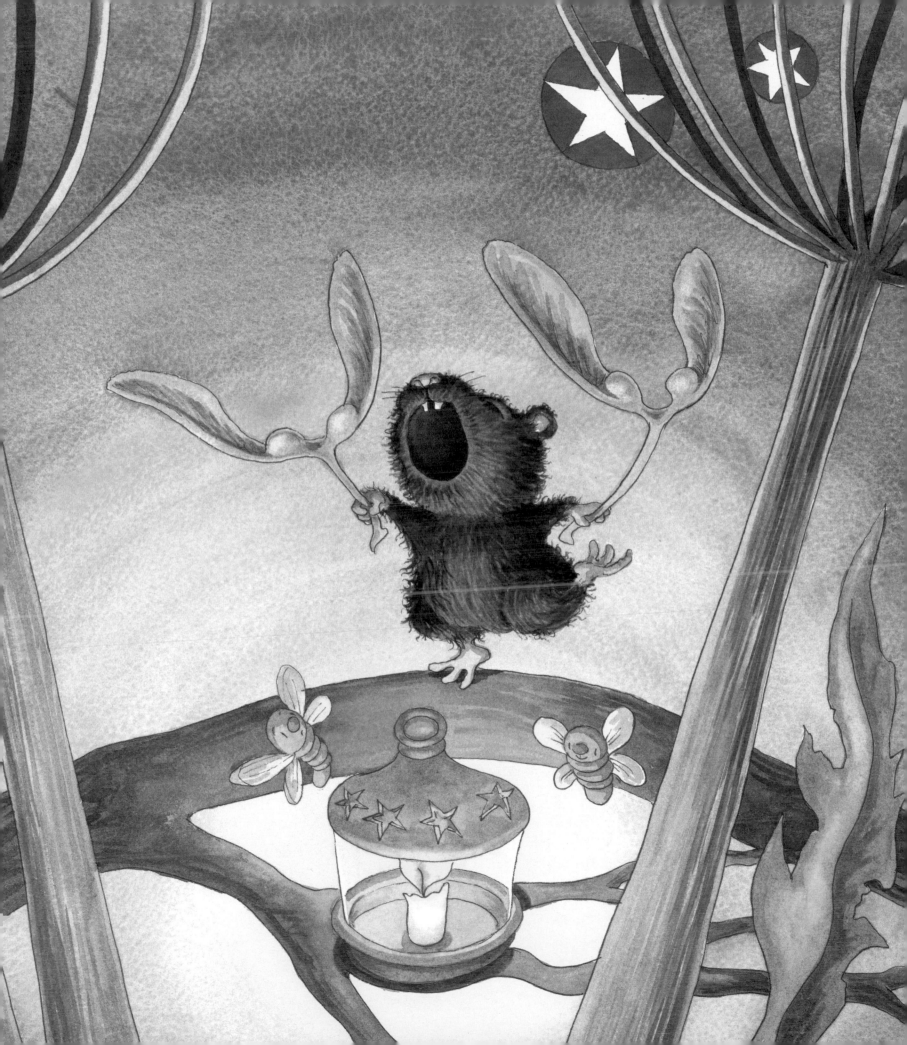

Oh! This was her other!

They'd make a great pair!

If only she'd noticed –

he'd always been there!

And now that they'd met,

there was so much to do.

They could do all the things

you can do as a two!

They could see-saw,

play catch,

and sit back to back.

They could hide in their den and share a nice snack.

They could sit and hold paws until daylight was gone.

Yes! Two little tails are much better than one.

They were peas in a pod. They were birds of a feather.

They were always best friends – whatever the weather.

Two wonderful ones had found a forever,
and forever is great when you spend it together.

And now, side by side, they heard the same tune,
so they sang to the stars and they danced to the moon.

Yes, deep in the heart of
Wintermouse Wood,
a friend by your side
makes life twice as good.

For my side-by-siders. You make life double wonderful – R.B.

For near friends, far friends,
new friends, old friends, and friends-to-be;
this one's for you with love – D.G.

First published in Great Britain in 2015 by Orchard Books London

ISBN 978-0-545-87215-7

12 11 10 9 8 7 6 5 4 3 2 1   15 16 17 18 19 20/0

Printed in the U.S.A.   08

First Scholastic paperback printing, September 2015